An Ancient Tale from India

Rama and the Demon King

Retold and illustrated by Jessica Souhami

DK INK • NewYork

This is the story of a brave and good prince called Rama, who should have been the happiest of men.

After all, he was the King's favorite son. He had a dear wife called Sita, and he had the best of friends in his brother, Lakshman.

And all the people in the kingdom loved him.

Well, all but one . . .
and that was his jealous stepmother.

She HATED Rama.

And she planned to get rid of him forever.

So she set a trap. . . .

Rama's wicked stepmother went to the King.

"Long ago," she said, "I saved your life and you promised to grant me any wish. Now I want you to send Rama into the forest for fourteen years."

The King was horrified. The forest was full of terrible demons. But what could he do?

A king MUST keep his promise.

With a broken heart, he sent Rama away.

But Sita and Lakshman would not let Rama go alone. So that very day, all three left the palace to face the dangers of the forest together.

In the forest, news of Rama's exile spread fast.

The demons hated anyone good and they were looking for a fight. As soon as Rama, Sita, and Lakshman appeared, the demons attacked them gleefully.

But both princes were brilliant fighters. They fought back bravely and killed thousands of demons until, at last, there was peace in the forest.

Rama, Sita, and Lakshman built a house, gathered fruit and berries for food, and lived a quiet and simple life among the forest animals.

But it was not to last.

Far away, in a magnificent palace on the island of Lanka, lived Ravana, the ten-headed king of all the demons.

He was evil and proud.

"No one can defeat me," he boasted. "No one is stronger. No one is more cunning. No one knows as much magic."

He smiled ten horrible smiles.

One day, a messenger arrived from India and told Ravana how Rama and Lakshman had killed thousands of his demons.

"WHAAAAT!!" his ten mouths screeched.

And he quivered with rage.

Ravana leapt into his magic chariot and flew to India. There he hid in a tree, ready to pounce on Rama and Lakshman.

But when he caught sight of Sita, he stopped short, dazzled by her beauty.

"She must be my queen!" he muttered. "I'll steal her from Rama and leave him brokenhearted. That will serve him right for killing my demons!"

And his ten brains buzzed with evil schemes.

This is what Ravana did.

He sent a magic deer into the forest, a golden creature that enchanted Sita. But whenever she tried to stroke it, it moved just out of reach.

Rama offered to catch it for her.

"Lakshman," he said, "look after Sita while I'm gone. There may still be demons about."

And he followed the deer until they both disappeared from view.

All was quiet.

Suddenly, Sita and Lakshman heard a cry.

"Help me! Help me, Lakshman!"

It sounded just like Rama.

What should Lakshman do?

He could not look for Rama. He had to protect Sita.

But Sita said, "Leave me, Lakshman, and rescue Rama. I'm safe here. Hurry!"

Then Lakshman ran as fast as he could toward the voice.

But, of course, it was not Rama calling.

It was a fiendish trick of Ravana's.

And now Sita was alone.

Wicked Ravana swooped down and carried her off in his magic chariot.

Meanwhile, Lakshman found Rama unhurt. With horror, the brothers realized they had been tricked.

They raced back to Sita.

But she was gone.

Rama was desolate.

The two brothers looked for Sita all over India.
Their search seemed hopeless.

Then one day they came to the land of the monkeys.
There they met Hanuman, the leader of the monkey army,
and told him their story.

"Ravana has taken Sita," said Hanuman. "We saw them
flying toward his palace on the island of Lanka."

"But how can we reach her?" asked Rama. "The sea round
Lanka is full of monsters."

"I think I can help you," said Hanuman. "My father is Vayu, the Wind God, and so I can fly like the wind! I will find Sita for you."

Rama and Lakshman were astonished.

"Take my ring," said Rama. "When you find Sita, give it to her so she will know I sent you. Good luck."

And Hanuman flew across the treacherous sea to Lanka.

Hanuman found Sita imprisoned in Ravana's garden.

He gave her Rama's ring.

"I'm so glad to see you," she cried. "I've refused to become Ravana's queen. If I don't change my mind, he says he will chop me into little pieces and eat me up for breakfast!"

"Be brave, Sita," whispered Hanuman. "We will be back for you soon."

Hanuman returned to Rama with his news, and the monkey army prepared for battle.

They began by building an amazing bridge that stretched right across the sea from India to Lanka.

Then the army, led by Rama, Lakshman, and Hanuman, marched across it!

Ravana's demon army was waiting for them on Lanka.
A terrible battle began.

The demons tried all their evil tricks.

Some used magic arrows that turned into poisonous
snakes. Others became invisible, so that the monkeys saw
only a sea of whirling weapons. There were giant demons
with enormous strength and demons who could move at
the speed of light.

But Rama, Lakshman, and the monkey army stood
firm, and after many days of fierce fighting, the demons
were defeated.

BUT THEN . . .

Ravana appeared, his twenty eyes blazing.

"Ha, Rama!" he sneered. "You know you cannot beat ME!"

Rama was silent. He slowly raised his bow and released a magic arrow.

It found its own way to Ravana. It pierced his evil body. Ravana was DEAD.

Rama and Sita were reunited and they returned to India. Sadness overshadowed the land, for Rama's father had died of grief on the day they left the palace. But now the people rejoiced that Rama was home.

Rama was made king, with Sita his queen, and Lakshman and Hanuman at his side.

The celebrations lasted a whole month.

Even the stepmother who had plotted against Rama was invited.

Rama ruled wisely and well.

The land became fruitful, and at last the kingdom was free from all evil.

The story of Rama, who rescues his wife, Sita,
from the Demon King, has been told in India for thousands of years
and it is said to confer a blessing on all who hear it.
The legend may have been based on historical fact.
It was passed from person to person until, in about 400 B.C.,
the poet Valmiki wrote *The Ramayana*. Almost every regional language
in India has its own version, and the story has spread throughout
southeast Asia. Heroic saga, love story, and symbolic account
of the battle between good and evil, *The Ramayana* has
inspired countless works of art and literature.

A DK INK BOOK

First American Edition 1997
2 4 6 8 10 9 7 5 3 1

Published in the United States by
DK Publishing, Inc., 95 Madison Avenue
New York, NY 10016
Visit us on the World Wide Web at http://www.dk.com

Text, illustrations, and design copyright © 1997 by Jessica Souhami and Paul McAlinden

Library of Congress cataloging is available upon request.

ISBN 0-7894-2450-9

Printed in Hong Kong